THE MISSING CLUE

Emma Fischel

Illustrated by Adrienne Kern

Series Editor: Gaby Waters
Assistant Editor: Michelle Bates

Contents

This is an exciting detective story that you can solve yourself. Clues and evidence are lurking on almost every page, but stay alert for red herrings that might put you off the trail. Vital information may be hidden anywhere, so make sure you read the text carefully. Look closely at the pictures and study all the documents and messages.

At various points in the book you will find this symbol 🔍. When you see it, you can refer to the Detective Guide on page 48 for extra help. The guide will point you in the right direction and give you handy hints to help work out the mystery. By the end of page 43, you will have all the information you need to solve the case before all is finally revealed.

Good News

Hands trembling, Jack opened the package that had just arrived. He gasped. It was almost too good to be true. The first competition he had ever entered – and he had won!

His head spun as he read the details of the prize. For as long as he could remember, he had wanted to be a reporter. Now here was his big chance. And, who could tell, there might be a major story out there, just waiting to break . . .

Monday, October 5

CONGRATULATIONS, JACK!

You are the lucky winner of the CELEBRITY CHOMPERS competition!

We showed you six close-ups of celebrity mouths munching on TV Snax and asked you to name the stars. The only clue we gave you was that they were all up for Bravo awards this year. We also asked you to complete a tie-breaking slogan.

You, Jack, not only identified all the stars correctly but, in the opinion of our judges, yours was the best tie-breaking slogan!

Congratulations again, Jack! Now read on – and enjoy the prizes!

THE PRIZES!

Just look at what you have won, Jack!

A week as trainee reporter on Los Tamillion Informer, starting from Tuesday, October 20. Learn the ropes under the kindly guidance of Ed Lines, famous editor of Los Tamillion's number one TV mag. And – an added bonus – it will be during the week of the Bravos awards ceremony.

BUT THAT'S NOT ALL! You have also won

year's supply of TV Snax!
ear's free TV viewing!

ND THERE'S MORE! We are enclosing

A TV Snax badge printed with your prize-winning slogan!
A free copy of last week's issue of the Informer!
A replica of the Bravos award so coveted by TV's greatest stars, perfect in every detail!

The CELEBRITY CHOMPERS competition was a joint promotion from the makers of TV Snax, the Los Tamillion Informer and the Bravos Committee.

TV Snax	The number one TV nibble lurking in everybody's kitchen!
The Informer	The ground-breaking weekly TV news and views mag. Wednesday isn't complete without it!
The Bravos	TV's most important award ceremony, attended by TV's most glittering stars!

The esteemed panel of judges scrutinize the thousands of competition entries that flood in. From left to right: Kris P. Nibble of TV Snax, Ed Lines of the Informer, Billy Banter, famous host of the Bravos.

Destination Downtown

Downtown Central station on a gloomy autumn morning . . . The rain bounced off the grimy streets like stray bullets off a tin can. A hungry cat scavenged for food among the bins. A car prowled slowly by, while, huddled in a doorway, Jack saw a solitary figure turn up his collar against the cold.

Outside the station, Jack hesitated. Could this really be the right place? Then, buttoning his jacket tightly and clutching his map, he set off down Ambition Avenue to find the offices of the Informer. A man scurried past him, umbrella pulled down low over his face to keep out the driving rain.

The street curved sharply to the right. Around the bend a grubby nameplate announced number 1013. This was it, and the door was already open. Inside, an iron staircase spiralled upward to a dusty skylight way above. Jack's feet echoed loudly on the worn stone steps as he made his way to the third floor.

The Informer office seemed a busy place. No one heard Jack knock and no one noticed as he pushed open the door and stood, dripping, in the doorway. After a moment he coughed politely, then coughed again, this time a little louder.

At last a woman swathed in lilac turned her head. "Yes?" she said, tucking a pencil neatly behind one ear.

"I-I-I'm the competition winner," Jack said nervously. "When hunger attacks, reach for TV Snax . . . I'm here for a week as my prize."

"Is that so?" said the lilac vision, scrutinizing Jack from head to foot. "You'd better see the boss, then. The door over there," she said, jerking a finger in the direction of the far end of the room. "Knock, then wait. Oh," she added. "And good luck . . ."

About the Informer

Ed Lines, ace newshound, glared out at Jack from behind a cluttered desk. "So you want to be a reporter," barked the famous journalist. "Well, let me tell you, you're starting at the top with the Informer!"

With that, the magazine mogul eased himself out of his swivel chair and strode over to a vast portrait hanging prominently on the wall.

"Mother," he announced proudly. "She created the Informer. She dreamed of building the greatest magazine ever about television and its stars – the best articles, best photos, best everything. And she did it! From the very first issue, she got all the major scoops and stories. No other paper could compete."

"And it all started from here almost thirty years ago," continued the media tycoon, slapping his hand down hard on his battered old desk. "We've never moved since. Everything is still just the way mother had it."

"But fifteen years ago mother was called to the great gossip column in the sky," said Ed. He paused to blow his nose vigorously, then continued. "I took over. For years I have dreamed of handing the Informer down the generations, but it seems destined not to be."

Dabbing at his eyes, Ed Lines rummaged about in a drawer. "Here. Read this," he said, handing Jack a bulky document.

THE INFORMER

The Informer, founded 27 years ago, quickly established itself as the number one magazine for television news and gossip. A weekly magazine that comes out every Wednesday, it is still widely read today. It was the brainchild of Isabel Lines, widow of Alfie Lines, the famous ventriloquist. Isabel founded the magazine at the age of 50, encouraged by her children, Edmund (then 20) and Christabel (then 15). The first issue was an instant sell-out, breaking the story of the split of two of the most famous TV stars of the day.

Isabel Lines died at the age of 62. Her son, Edmund, took over as editor of the Informer and continues today, 15 years later. The Informer still operates from the same offices of its humble beginnings in the Downtown Central district. In an interview just before her death, Isabel Lines confessed to her dream of the Informer carrying on as a family-run business, but sadly, it seems the Lines dynasty is not destined to continue.

Very first issue

Family trouble

Fifteen years ago Edmund's sister, Christabel, cut all contact with her brother. This followed a fight over her refusal to join the Informer on the death of their mother. After 11 years of silence Christabel wrote to Edmund from far-off Mythika, telling him he was now uncle to a three-year-old girl and suggesting a reunion. Tragically, that was the last Edmund heard from her. He has since had no success in tracing her.

Edmund's daughter, Arabella (from his marriage to actress Posy Bouquet), chose to follow her mother into the acting profession. She shows no interest in taking up the leadership of the Informer. Because of this, she and her father no longer speak to each other.

Isabel Lines with her children 20 years ago

Biggest scoop

Ten years ago the Informer broke all circulation records with photos of top star Drusilla Dazzle in a dramatic drenching incident. It stemmed from Ms. Dazzle's involvement with the ill-fated musical tragedy, Dreamaway. On the opening night her co-star was taken ill and the understudy, Bob Swing, took over. But he ruined the play by forgetting his lines and altering the course of the plot, throwing the rest of the cast into complete confusion.

The critics savaged the play and it closed after one night. Drusilla used her influence to ensure Swing would never work in Los Tamillion again. Some months later, he burst into the restaurant where Drusilla was dining. He stormed up to her table and emptied the contents of a flower vase over her head, then left town, vowing revenge. An Informer photographer on the spot got exclusive pictures of the whole incident and the public flocked to buy copies. It became the Informer's biggest selling issue.

Biggest seller ever

A Lucky Break

R-r-ring! The shrill noise of the phone cut through the silence in the room. "Yup," said Ed tersely into the receiver. "What! No . . . how long? Disaster!" With that he hung up, scowling.

"So you want to be a reporter?" he said again. "Well, here's your chance. May Kittup, our star reporter, has just broken her toe. She won't be in for a while and no one else is free to take over her story. It's about Workout. We want a story on the show to tie in with the Bravos."

To: May Kittup
From: Ed Lines
Date: October 13

Ten days to the Bravos. We need a story for our bumper Bravos issue. Suggest you get down to Qualivision and do a feature on Workout and the Bravos. Interview the stars that are up for awards, find out about Workout's past wins and losses, see what preparations they are making for the ceremony. Get me any information you can.

Have attached a few recent bits of info which may help. Report in to me with progress each morning.

Good luck!

Qualivision — the TV channel that brings you hits such as Workout, Timeshare and Teen Trivia from its Los Tamillion Studios.

Sam Smarm, publicity department.

TV in a class of its own!

Qualivision TV studios
1-111 Media Mile
Los Tamillion West

BRAVO MANIA!

It's that time of year again, when the nation tunes in to see who will win – and lose – TV's most coveted awards. On Friday, October 23 at 7pm, two hours of awards and entertainment will be broadcast live to millions of homes around the globe. Yes, it's Bravo time once again!

Fraser Storey, last year's winner for Best Play, Backstabbers. Said Fraser: "For 10 years I've dreamed of winning a Bravo – but I never expected it would be for writing!"

A win can transform a career. Last year, Fraser Storey (pictured above) found his dreams came true after his win for TV drama. Previously a complete unknown, the next day he was offered a plum script-writing job for Workout, TV's highest rated soap.

* SHOW NEWS * SHOW NEWS * SHOW NEWS * SHOW NEWS *

WORKOUT - TWO YEARS ON TOP!

TV's highest rated soap is coming to the end of its second great year. And the number one from Qualivision is also up for five Bravos to add to the three it has already. That's more nominations than any other show!

It is almost two years since viewers first tuned in to the comings and goings of everyday life in a busy sports and leisure complex. The show has since become an institution, capturing the imagination of the public and touching the hearts of millions. Will Coach leave for pastures new? Will Dan ever forgive Daisy? All these and more are questions the public wants answered. And they will be, so keep tuning in!

Rock Solid plays Coach

Luke Martin plays Dan

NOW MEET THE STARS!

The stalwarts, with us from the beginning and – we hope – to the end, need no introduction
Rock Solid, known to millions of viewers simply as "Coach".
Luke Martin, idol to young people everywhere as athlete Dan Drummond.

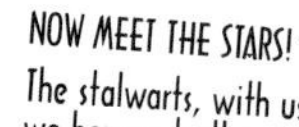

Drusilla Dazzle plays Billie

Bella Bouquet plays Anna

Hello to our newest recruits, bringing fresh life to the show in October:
Drusilla Dazzle plays ferocious new owner of the Workout complex, Billie O'Nair.
Bella Bouquet plays her fresh and lovely young assistant, Anna Peel.

And last but not least, that famous feline friend of the viewers, *Pawprint*. A true star – and he behaves like one! He will eat only Meaty Morsels (Chunky variety) and lies only on a patterned silk rug, which must always be tucked in the same way before he will sleep on it.

"First thing to do is show the Workout team the photos we took at Friday's rehearsals. They have to approve them before we use them," Ed continued. "Then find out all you can about Workout and the Bravos." He handed Jack an envelope. "This should help start you off."

Jack opened the envelope. There were the four photos, plus a couple of newspaper articles. Workout . . . the Bravos . . . what a combination – TV's number one soap and the biggest awards ceremony known to the world of television!

September 30

HIJACKED

Soap war bubbles over! Shock double move by Dru and Bella!

Dru and Bella go out to celebrate newly signed contracts with Qualivision.

Goodbye Terminal! We're off to Workout.

Drusilla Dazzle and Bella Bouquet today announced their departure from Terminal, the popular twice weekly soap about life in a busy airport. They move next week to Workout, which recently nudged Terminal into the number two position in the TV soap war. Both stars deny any truth in reports of constant battles on the soap set over who has the greater number of lines, more close-ups and better scenes. Said Drusilla last night, "Bella and I are good friends. Don't believe everything you read!"

TUG-OF-LOVE MINNIE TIPPED FOR TOP

Minnie Marvel is tipped for an award at this week's Bravos for her portrayal of tug-of-love Viola in Workout. The nomination has a tragic poignancy, as in real life little Minnie is an orphan. Four years ago, Minnie and her mother were kidnap victims. One of the kidnap gang, struck by remorse, helped them escape but, tragically, her mother fell over a cliff.

Plucky little Minnie doesn't remember much about it. "We were kept in a dark, smelly room. A nice man helped us escape. When mother fell over he carried me to safety along a tree branch wedged on the waterfall. I was scared. It was very high and the branch was very narrow, but he didn't seem to mind at all."

Minnie's father never recovered from the loss of his wife and soon passed away. His step-sister, Cosima Charade, took Minnie in. "Minnie begged me to let her go on the stage," says her devoted guardian. "And after all she had been through, how could I refuse?" How fitting that little Minnie is now in line for a major TV award. What a worthy winner!

Inside Qualivision

The train screeched to a halt. Through the window Jack could see the station sign: Media Mile. This was the stop for Qualivision. The train doors opened with a hiss and Jack got off.

Outside, the skyline was dominated by a huge building that stretched way down the street. Hundreds of windows glinted in the feeble rays of the winter sun. Jack clutched the envelope Ed had given him tightly to his chest and headed for a revolving door set high up a wide stone staircase. He pushed the door open and stepped inside the headquarters of Qualivision, the most famous TV studio in Los Tamillion . . .

Jack's shoes squeaked loudly with every step he took across the vast expanse of marble flooring. He arrived at the reception desk in the corner. "Excuse me," he stuttered, nervously. "I'm looking for the Workout studio."

"Guided tours every Tuesday, two o'clock," droned the receptionist.

"N-no," stumbled Jack. "I'm here on business . . . from the Informer. I'm expected. I –"

"You'll need to see Thea Trickell, then," interrupted the receptionist. "She's in charge."

"How do I find her?" asked Jack.

"Try turning around," said the receptionist, pointing her expertly manicured finger in the direction of the sofa.

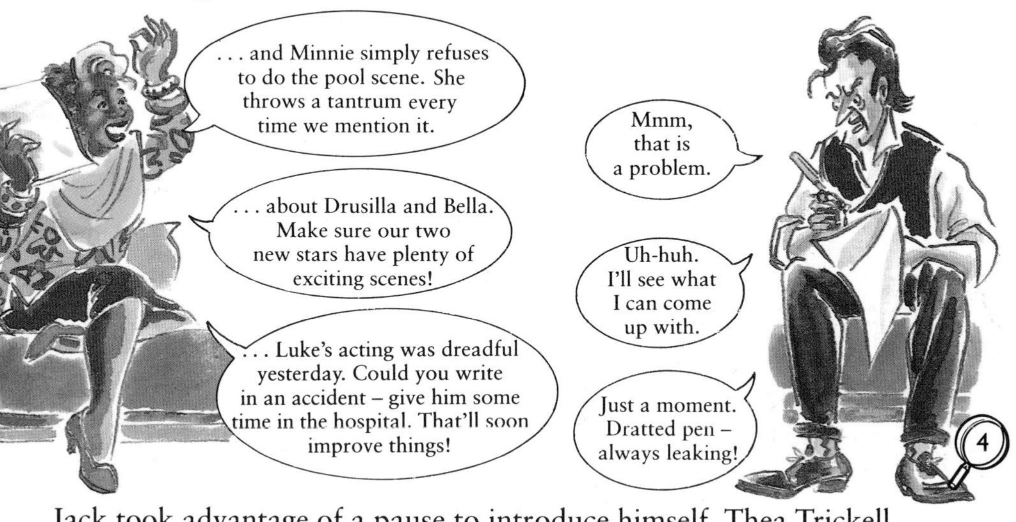

Jack took advantage of a pause to introduce himself. Thea Trickell leaped up. "Splendid!" she said. "Come and show everyone the photos." Heels clicking busily on the floor, she swept out of the hall, talking hard. "Let me tell you a bit about us," she said. "I am producer and director of Workout."

"Which means she runs the whole show," interrupted the man with the leaking pen, panting in her wake. "Anything she says goes."

"That's Fraser Storey," said Thea beaming. "He writes each episode." Then she stopped outside a door.

Behind the Scenes

Thea Trickell took a deep breath. "Attention!" she roared. Awestruck, Jack watched the stars immediately form an obedient group around their leader. "Three days to go to the Bravos," began Thea. "And I have some exciting news. The organizers have asked us to perform a short scene during the ceremony. It will be seen around the globe in thousands of countries. This means worldwide publicity for Workout."

"Over the next few days press interest will be high," continued Thea. Then she turned to Jack with a smile . . .

"And, of course, there's Drusilla Dazzle," added Thea. "But she's out representing Workout at a theme park opening today."

"Jack is researching an article on Workout to tie in with the Bravos," Thea continued. "Please give him all the help you can. First, he has some photos for you all to look at." Jack handed them around.

"Enough!" said Thea briskly. "To work. We need to rehearse the new scene for the Bravos. Remember, only three more days to go."

6

A Busy Day

Fraser Storey handed each of the actors a copy of the short scene he had written for the Bravos ceremony. He started to speak. "Right, here's what happens. We start with Minnie alone on stage. She's playing with a boxing glove. All of a sudden, Coach bursts in. He's agitated beyond belief . . ."

Fraser waved his pen back and forth as he outlined the scene. Red ink leaked from the nib and dribbled down his arm but he seemed not to notice. "Then – wham! – the curtain comes down," he finished triumphantly.

"Marvellous!" exclaimed Thea. "Let's read the scene through. I'll take Drusilla's lines." And so the first rehearsal began.

From a seat in the corner of the studio, Jack watched the rehearsal speed by. Then he queued with the actors for lunch in the Qualivision canteen.

Precisely forty-five minutes later everyone was back in the studio. Rehearsals continued for an hour, then a rail of glamorous clothes was wheeled in through the door. "Time to choose an outfit for the Bravos," said Thea to the cast. "You can take your pick from any of these clothes, courtesy of Qualivision."

Decisions proved hard to make but at last everyone was satisfied they had found the perfect outfit for the great occasion. "Five o'clock," announced Thea. "That's it for now. Time to go home."

Ten minutes later, Rock was the first to go. Bella and Luke left soon after him, followed swiftly by Minnie and her guardian. Then Thea looked at her watch and gasped, "Five-twenty. I must dash!"

Jack picked up the envelope Ed Lines had given him. It felt light – very light. Puzzled, he pushed his hand inside the flap. Where were the photos?

What can I do? he thought, quaking. And what on earth will Ed Lines say when he hears I've lost the photos?

Lost and Found

At last Ed Lines ran out of insults. "This is not a good start to your second day," he snarled. Grabbing a grubby folder from his desk, he started to leaf through the pages inside. "OK Office Supplies . . . Pablo's Pasta . . . It's in here somewhere," he muttered. "Ah-hah! 'Paparazzi Printers. Open nine to five, seven days a week.' That's the one."

"They printed the photos," Ed explained. "They still have the negatives, so we can get copies." With that, he picked up the phone and dialled. Minutes later he slammed the phone down. "We're too late," he said, perplexed. "Someone went there yesterday – said they were from Qualivision and needed the negatives of the Workout session. The printers never thought to question them."

"Whoever it was must have seen the printers' name stamped on the back of the photos," Ed mused.

Then Ed stopped, interrupted by a sudden cough from the doorway . . .

Ed Lines got out two large cigars. "So what brings you over this way, Will?" he asked the craggy-faced private eye.

"Big trouble, Ed," sighed Will Pry. "I need your help, and fast. Remember this?" He slapped a piece of paper down on the desk . . .

the names
tv stars
offspring?
our survey
can reveal
this year
popular
for girls:

Whimsie
Sparkle
Porcelain
Chiffon
Pizazz
Moonshine
Starlette
Cosmos
Vitality
Beluga
Eternity
Shimmer
Blushes
Chemise
Alopecia
Pomegranate

WHERE ARE THEY NOW?

This week we ask for your help in tracking down a bunch of ruthless criminals known as the Spotlight Gang. Over the last few years, a wave of seamy showbiz crimes has shocked the citizens of Los Tamillion. Remember the Mogul Mansion burglary, the Dynamite Duo kidnapping, the Replica Ruby blackmail case? The Spotlight Gang is believed to be responsible for them all!

The gang's roots can be traced back at least four years. Their first known victims were child star Minnie Marvel (while still an unknown) and her mother, kidnapped in a tragic case of mistaken identity. The gang snatched the unlucky pair outside a museum in Mythika, believing them to be glamorous star Iva Bigg-Brake and her daughter, Ava. Upon discovering their mistake, they decided to dispose of the two in the Intrepid River, but were foiled by a member of the gang who has since disappeared.

Since that early bungled attempt, the Spotlight Gang has become increasingly dangerous. They need to be stopped! Our sources now believe that they are closer to rounding up the gang than ever before. But they need your help to make the streets of Los Tamillion safer for us all. Does this picture jog any memories? If you have any information, please contact us. Our office is waiting for your call!

continued from page 7.

also a child, who would now be seven. The only real clue we have lies in a letter, written from Mythika four years ago. It was the last letter ever received from her. Below we print an extract from it. Anyone with any information should contact the Missing Persons Hotline.

-3-

...can't imagine. I rushed out of the house to see her, drenched, with the empty bucket wedged on her head and her left arm stuck in the guttering. She said she had been trying to find out about the crime. Still, the scar (a strange kind of crescent shape) should fade with time. And I'm sure she'll get over her fears - at the moment she's so scared of water she even drinks through a straw! Anyway Ed, that's all my news. If you are prepared to let bygones be bygones and go along with my plans for a reunion, please contact me in Mythika. You and Archie will have so much in common and your little niece is longing to meet you.

All love, Christabel

"You ran this three weeks ago. Thanks to that we have new evidence," said Will Pry, pulling some photos out of his pocket. "We want to put these in every paper we can. They are from Elsa Storey, the eminent Mythikan plastic surgeon. By chance she saw that issue of the Informer, left by her brother over from Los Tamillion. She recognized the faces at once. It seems she did some work on the gang leader four years ago – these photos are after surgery. Elsa Storey says all but one of the gang had surgery of some kind. She was the perfect choice for their plans. She had just been abroad on a specialist course for three months, and hadn't heard about the kidnap. So she performed the surgery, not knowing she was helping wanted criminals. The gang then left Mythika and moved their crime base to Los Tamillion, complete with their new appearances, and free from fear of discovery."

"She has photos of them all before and after surgery, except one who changed his mind about treatment. She can't find his photo, although she knows she had one. A pity – but the leader is the one we really want."

Ed took the photos then turned to Jack. "Still here?" he barked. "Get down to Workout. And don't make any more mistakes!"

Superstar!

Outside the Qualivision building, Jack was startled by a sudden loud toot on a car horn. He jumped aside as a long black car with smoked glass windows screeched to a halt at the foot of the steps.

Drusilla Dazzle! Jack followed, awestruck, as the superstar swanned gracefully up the steps and into the Qualivision building.

"Flowers for you, Miss Dazzle," twittered the receptionist.

The glamorous star of stage and screen threw a sweeping glance around the hall. She caught sight of Jack hovering by the door and waved an imperious arm at him. "You there, bring them to my dressing room," she commanded.

Staggering under the weight of the enormous bouquet, Jack stood on the threshold of the star's dressing room. Drusilla Dazzle beckoned him in. "I daresay you want my autograph," she said, graciously. "Everyone does."

Picking up a leather-bound volume on her dressing table, the superstar smiled kindly at Jack. "I keep a store of photos tucked in here for my fans," she said. The book was full of old photos and press clippings. "My life has been a fairy tale," she sighed, lost in thought as she turned the pages. "Oh yes, I've had it all. Fame, fortune . . ."

Times were hard at first. Night after night in the chorus line. Then one evening fate took a hand – the star and understudy got food poisoning. I was pushed on stage to take over. That night was to change my life.

I became a star! Life was a glamorous whirl of parties, premières – and suitors. But I only had eyes for one man. Then came a hideous magazine article. Not one word was true, but the stubborn fool refused to listen. That was the last time we spoke. Nearly thirty years of silence . . .

Still my career scaled yet more glittering heights. I won award after award. My Etta in Showtime was hailed as a masterpiece, the best ever. Then came disaster, my first and last musical, Dreamaway. It closed after one night. But happier times were to follow – and another Bravo. How I wept!

The superstar dabbed at a tiny tear glistening in the corner of one eye. Just then, there was a rap on the door and a voice called out. "Drusilla, you're needed at the Bravos press interviews."

The Plot Thickens

Studio 3 was packed. Drusilla took her place on the podium while Jack squeezed into a seat at the back of the room. Then Thea started the press session. But events were soon to take a dramatic turn . . .

Bewildered, Jack watched as the Workout team, led by Luke, helped themselves to copies of the paper that had just landed in a thick bundle on the floor. What was Qualitime?

Thea saw his puzzled face and picked up an extra copy. "Take a look," she said, handing it to him. "Everyone at Qualivision reads it."

QUALITIME

The daily read for all Qualivision workers. Monday to Friday, Qualitime keeps you informed.

QUALIVISION, TV'S BEST AND BRIGHTEST CHANNEL

Today, a special word from Ivan Inkling, your managing director.

Greetings, everyone! This Friday sees a very special day – the thirtieth anniversary of the Bravos. Yes, the greatest of TV awards ceremony is upon us once again.

And each year, one of the most consistent presences, with winners galore, has been Qualivision! Let's hope this year turns out to be no exception.

To celebrate this thirtieth year of the Bravos, we look back at some past triumphs from Qualivision – and forward, we hope, to some future ones.

So, welcome to a special Bravos edition of Qualitime!

30 YEARS OF QUALIVISION AND THE BRAVOS

30 years of laughter and tears, winners and losers. We look back over some of our most successful Bravo years.

Year 1. Best comedy award: Rock Solid and Drusilla Dazzle in Qualivision's ***Hush my mouth!***

Year 20. Best actress: Drusilla Dazzle in Qualivision's ***Grit****.*

Year 29. Best TV drama: Qualivision's ***Backstabbers*** *(shown here in rehearsal).*

In the first year of the Bravos, Qualivision scooped best comedy award. Rock went on to star as Jed Slim, cowboy hero of the popular TV series, Gun Shy (repeated 20 years later and just as popular!). Drusilla had only recently shot to stardom, and was soon destined to become a household name, known to millions as Leila in Travesty, the long-running saga of the Midas family.

Drusilla wins again for Qualivision 20 years later for her no-holds-barred portrayal of wronged widow Faith Anhope. Qualivision's Grit, a tale of one woman's rise to fame, fortune and power against all the odds, came only months after she starred in the ill-fated Dreamaway. Dreamaway may have ruined the career of her co-star, Bob Swing, but Dru certainly managed to rise above it!

Best TV drama was one of a clutch of awards Qualivision gained last year. Just over a year ago Qualivision spotted Fraser Storey's potential and was brave enough to take a chance on an unknown. The reward was a searing drama of the backstage, backbiting world of the acting profession. Gossip raged as to who the characters were based on but our number one writer is not saying anything..!

In the canteen, nearly everyone was reading Qualitime. Jack browsed through his copy while he munched a sticky bun, on the lookout for information that might prove handy for his article . . .

Wednesday, October 21

170659

QUALIVISION, TV WITH GUTS

Today, a little reminder to you all. Successful though Qualivision is, we still have to watch those pennies! In the interest of Quali-conomy all phone calls are now logged, and have been for the past week. From now on, each department will get a daily list of all calls made. The list will show the time and length of the call, and the number called (including those made to other Qualivision departments). I shall examine these lists daily. So keep those calls short, and let's have no more time wasted chatting to friends in other departments or auntie in Ohio. You have been warned!

Time for our daily word from Jenny, Qualivision's general manager.

THIS YEAR'S HOPES

Qualivision has nominations in almost every category this year:

Best TV drama: No Way Out
Best comedy: Timeshare
Best daytime drama: Workout
Best children's presenter: Susie Slapstick
Best documentary: Beginners Please!
Best actor: Rock Solid
Best newcomer: Bella Bouquet
Best supporting actress: Minnie Marvel

And a special mention for Drusilla Dazzle who this year collects a Lifelong Devotion award, for her contribution to quality programming in the arts. Well deserved, Dru!

Best children's presenter, Susie Slapstick, wacky host of ***Splat!***

Best documentary: the first week for new pupils at Precocia Stage School.

PERSONAL

Puts you in touch with 9000 Quali-workers – or just one special person! Phone or deliver your ad to us by three o'clock to appear in the next issue of Qualitime.

For sale, flute, hardly used. Wanted, triangle.
Amelia. Return the lemon squeezer and no more will be said.
Good as new! Second-hand designer clothes at Catch a Falling Star.
Eat at Pearl's. Shellfish to the stars.
John. Make someone very happy. Give up the mandolin.
A new you! Elsa Storey, plastic surgeon to the rich and famous.
'Dan'. This time things are more complicated. Two jobs for you. New instructions in the same place. Don't fail me or you know what will happen.
Your portrait painted by Karen Dash, artist of quality.

QUIZTIME
What well-known scribe has a plastic surgeon sister?
What budding starlet has a news magnate father?
What major producer has a private eye stepson?
And what Bravo-nominated show connects them all?

Do you have the answers? If so, drop them into the office by four o'clock. First correct entry out of the bag wins a set of dumb-bells!

13

The rest of the day passed in a whirl. Jack asked question after question about Workout and its stars. By the end of the day his notepad was packed with scribbled information. At last, exhausted, he went home to bed.

In the News

The Informer office was practically deserted when Jack arrived the next morning. He switched on the battered old television in the corner and the morning's news stories began to filter quietly into the room. Settling himself at an empty desk, Jack opened his reporter's notepad and looked through his last two day's notes.

Workout
Goes out twice a week (Tuesdays and Thursdays at 7:30pm) on Qualivision.
Has been running for two years.
Actors get their scripts for each week on Tuesday morning. They rehearse and record from Tuesday to Sunday, 8am-5pm.
They have Mondays off.
(This week they came in on Monday as well because of preparing for the Bravos.)
They work on episodes two weeks ahead of the ones we see on TV.

Qualivision
TV channel which has been going for 33 years. All shows made by Qualivision studios.

Rock Solid
First appeared as a carrot in a commercial for Soupy Sauce Mix.
Made his name as Jed Slim in Gun Shy. Also films and stage work but career faded for a while when he got a reputation as unreliable after split with Drusilla Dazzle.
Did a lot of charity work for Broken Hearts Anonymous. Made a comeback when old episodes of Gun Shy reran 10 years ago. Suddenly became cult figure and in demand again. Landed part of Coach in Workout two years ago. Has been in show since first episode.

Luke Martin
First big break was as Ryan Keen in Kid Cop nearly 4 years ago.

Has played Dan Drummond in Workout since episode 10.
Before that, lot of travel to different countries - his parents were a circus trapeze and high wire act. Luke joined the act 6 years ago but left suddenly after 2 years and moved to Los Tamillion.
Only Workout star not in line for Bravo award.

Drusilla Dazzle
Has been almost constantly in work ever since pulled out of chorus line and made a star. Only flop in her career was Dreamaway.
Has taught regular acting classes at Would-Beez Academy for Young Actors for nearly 10 years.
Says she knows she has been fortunate and hopes she can pass some of that good fortune by helping young actors learn their craft properly.
Is frightened of small dogs.

Bella Bouquet
Grew up in Los Tamillion. Always wanted to be an actress but strong opposition from her father.
Took various jobs to put herself through drama college. Has not spoken to father for two years.
First stage job two years ago. First TV was Terminal. Moved to Workout at same time as Drusilla Dazzle, two weeks ago.
Likes hot air ballooning.
Does voluntary work for Missing Persons Hotline.

Things to find out
Ask Fraser how he gets ideas for plot. When did he start writing? What made him start? What did he do before?
See if Thea will tell me more about stars. Things like who is easy to work with, who is difficult; who gets along with whom; are there many arguments between actors? And anything else she can think of.

Jack sighed. Being a reporter was not as easy as it seemed. He had plenty of information, but where was the story to go with it? If only something really interesting would happen –

Suddenly Jack looked up at the television. Something the newscaster was saying had caught his attention . . .

News is coming in of a ramatic collapse on by a member of cast of Workout. We have no more details as yet.
Wait a moment . . . I think, yes . . . we can now go over to Qualivision, where our reporter is first on the scene.
Errr, we, err, seem unable to . . . Wait, I'm getting . . . Yes, we are now able to bring you that report, from Carlotta Fibbs, our woman on the scene.
Well, Mike, the scene here outside the Qualivision studios is chaos.
It seems that, in a tragic piece of bad luck, one of the cast of Workout died just ten minutes ago, seemingly the victim of some kind of poison.
And yes, a stretcher is appearing. I can't quite see . . . could it be carrying the unidentified tragic TV star?
Sobbing fans line the street, waiting for a glimpse of their stricken hero. No one knows who the victim is. Back to you in the studio, Mike.
We will of course bring you more news on that story later.

A Tragic Tale

There was no time to waste. Jack was out of the door and heading for the station in seconds. This is it, he thought, as he bounded aboard an uptown train. My first scoop! But he was not the only one on the trail of the story . . .

A crowd thronged the Qualivision steps. How would Jack ever get through? Just then he heard a familiar voice behind him. It was Will Pry! The private eye propelled Jack to the front of the crowd.

Seconds later, the guard waved them inside. "I found his lost parakeet," explained Will tersely. He sprinted along the maze of corridors that led to studio 3. Then he pushed open the door.

"Then Pawprint lapped up the spilled liquid," finished Thea. "And, two minutes later, he died." She blew her nose loudly. "They've just carried him into the ambulance. Now all that's left is an empty basket."

Fraser patted her arm, then moved over to the abandoned basket. "It's too sad a reminder. It's upsetting you, I'll move it," he said kindly.

"Stop right there!" ordered Will Pry. "Where are the actors? I need statements from everyone."

Thea sniffed. "They all went to their dressing rooms. At least, I know Bella and Drusilla did. They're very shocked."

Will turned to Jack. "You stay here. Remember – no one touches anything!" Then the three of them left.

Jack heard a scrabbling noise in the roof. Rats, he thought, shivering. It was eerie to be alone in the studio . . . But was he?

Minnie Steps In

Jack spun around to see Minnie Marvel beckoning mysteriously. "Follow me," she said. "I may have a clue about the poisoner." With that, she headed off for a corner of the studio.

Perplexed, Jack followed her. "I want to be a crime reporter," explained Minnie, "so I'm gathering evidence for my first big story. I haven't got the answer yet. But there seem to be plenty of suspects," she added darkly.

What was she talking about? thought Jack, confused. Then, dimly, he heard more rustling from the roof. Those rats again . . .

"I hate being an actress," sighed the chattering child star. Suddenly she slithered underneath a rail of clothes tucked away in a dark corner.

"Cosima put me on the stage," Minnie's voice continued, muffled, from under the rail. "She's my guardian, my father's step-sister. There's no one else to look after me. Well, I think my mother had a brother but they didn't speak." Then she emerged, flushed with success and clutching a small suitcase.

There was a loud bang as the studio door shut. But surely it had been shut already – could it have blown open?

After a moment Minnie continued. "This is my evidence box," she announced, brandishing the battered old suitcase with pride. Then she clicked open the lid.

Amazed, Jack peered inside at an array of things belonging to the Workout team. For a moment he hesitated, then he started to read. It's a reporter's duty not to overlook information that comes his way, he told himself firmly. It's how you use it that matters.

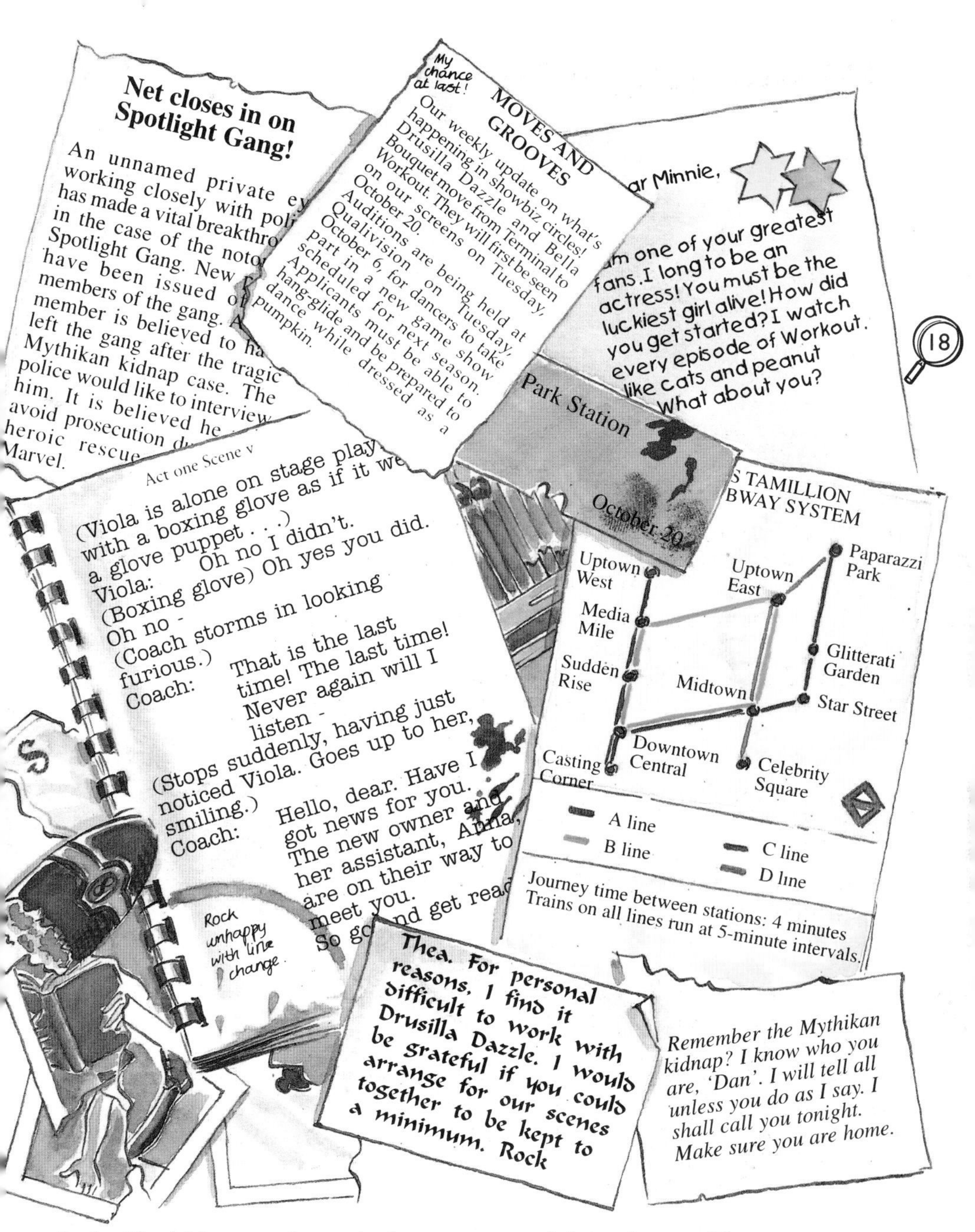

Jack sifted his way through the contents of the suitcase. There was plenty to read and at the bottom of the pile, he found some scraps of glossy paper. There was something familiar about them. He pulled them out for a closer look . . . the missing photos, torn up! Just then, the studio door creaked open.

More Shocks in Store

Through the doorway came a giant bouquet, carried by a staggering delivery boy. Another followed, and then another. By two o'clock Pawprint's basket was surrounded by tributes from a devastated public who had by now heard the ghastly details of his death by poison.

Then the Workout team arrived. Shocked and distressed, they were all still unable to talk about anything but Pawprint's tragic demise.

"Never liked the critter but never wished him harm," sniffed Rock.
"A poisoner among us? Surely not!" said Drusilla.
"How could anyone be so cruel?" wept Bella.
"If only he hadn't drunk it," sighed Luke.

For a moment there was silence. Everyone stared sadly at the shrine to the feline fatality, then Thea gathered herself together. "We must put this behind us," she said bracingly. "The show must go on. Think of the Bravos. It's what Pawprint would have wanted."

While preparations got under way for the rehearsal, Will Pry beckoned to Jack. "I found some interesting things just now, kid," said the private eye. "But I need more evidence. We're dealing with a major star here." The sleuth put a heavy hand on Jack's shoulder. "Problem is, I have another big case at the moment. I need you to . . ."

He was just about to say more when Thea called for silence. And so work began again on the ill-fated scene that had led to Pawprint's untimely death. For a few minutes things went smoothly, until . . .

Crrrk! A heavy arc light creaked ominously above the Workout team. Seconds later, it hurtled down from the ceiling. For one terrible moment it seemed certain to the horrified onlookers that Bella would be crushed beneath it. Then Fraser Storey, in a lightning-quick move, pushed her out of the way. The light whistled past her head and crashed to the ground.

"I could have been killed," gasped Bella. She lay sprawled on the floor, deathly pale.

Will Pry spoke. "Something mighty strange is going on around here. This makes one narrow escape too many. It's time to act!"

A Falling Star

Will Pry knelt down and examined the light closely, muttering under his breath. Then he stood up and made a startling pronouncement. "This was no accident. This was a cold-blooded attempt at murder!" Amid gasps of disbelief from every corner of the studio, Will Pry continued. "The metal ropes have been part-sawn through. This is the latest in a whole series of attempts on the life of an innocent young girl."

"In the first attempt," the private eye continued, "the lights fused. A lucky chance, or deliberate sabotage – who can say? But, whichever it was, someone seized the opportunity."

"The villain grabbed Bella, intending to strangle her, but lost courage. Fearing time would run out, the culprit ripped off the necklace to make it look like robbery." By now Will had everyone's complete attention. "The next time, careful planning went into the attempt," he said. "It was only Bella's problem with her lines and Fraser's intervention that saved her from Pawprint's fate."

"The villain was becoming desperate," continued Will Pry to his rapt audience. "The arc light was risky – there was no absolute guarantee it would land on Bella – but it was worth a try."

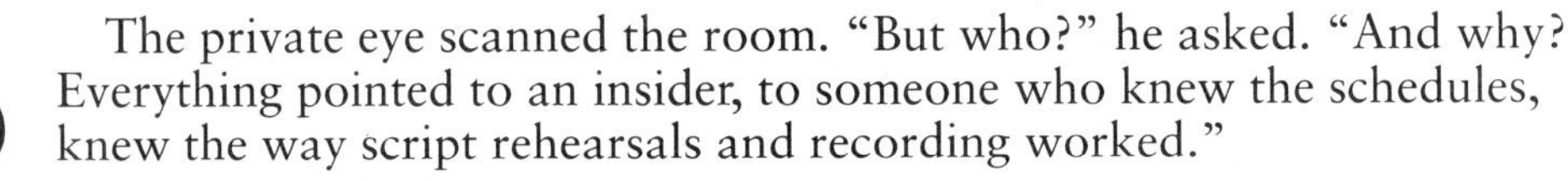

The private eye scanned the room. "But who?" he asked. "And why? Everything pointed to an insider, to someone who knew the schedules, knew the way script rehearsals and recording worked."

"I turned up some interesting finds," continued the sleuth. "A book on poisons. Fragments of a broken bottle bearing traces of tedium hypochondriade, a deadly substance when drunk. And, most significant of all, some broken metal rope, used by the villain to work out how far the ropes would need to be sawn to make them snap at the right time. All these things were in one dressing room. But whose?"

"You had me fooled to begin with, lady," Will Pry said to Drusilla. "I let you blind me to the truth. But no more! It was a sad case of professional jealousy turning to terrible crime. One star threatened by the meteoric rise of another – it's a common enough story in this town." Before anyone could respond, there was a loud rap on the door and four police officers walked in. Will Pry nodded in the direction of the dumbfounded star. "There's the culprit!" he said.

Handcuffed and chalky-faced, Drusilla was led away. Everyone stood, stunned, as the door swung gently to a close behind her. Something stirred at the back of Jack's mind. It was as if he had just been reminded of something important as he watched Drusilla leave. But what was it that had made his mind race? Just then, Will Pry's phone started to ring.

Uh-huh. Downtown stakeout. There in twenty minutes.

The private eye talked fast, then the conversation was over. "Kid," he said, turning to Jack. "Get back to the Informer. Let Ed know what's happened. And tell him, if all goes well, I may soon have a scoop for him on the Spotlight Gang." Will Pry headed for the door. "I gotta go," he said. "The net is closing on a truly wicked bunch of criminals." With that, he pulled his hat low over his brow and left.

Questions Galore

Ed was beside himself with excitement. "Tell me again," he urged. "From the fused lights to Drusilla's arrest. I want to hear it all!" Jack went through it once more.

"And Bella is unharmed, you say?" queried Ed anxiously. As Jack nodded he rubbed his hands with glee. "What a story! What a tie-in with the Bravos!"

Ed rushed happily back to his desk, but Jack was worried. It seemed to him that many of the things that had happened over the last few days just didn't add up. He wasn't convinced that Will Pry was right. But what could he do about it?

He sat down with a sigh. He felt something in his back pocket. The photos! Why not stick them back together, he mused, digging out all the scraps. After all, their disappearance was the first thing to happen in this strange saga.

Jack stared at the photos he had pieced back together. There were only three. He had a scrap from the corner of the fourth photo. But where was the rest of it? Things were getting more and more puzzling.

Jack's head was teeming with questions. Why would anyone steal the photos? Then why tear them up? What had been in the one that was missing? Was there something important about it? Could it have a link with everything that had happened since?

The more he thought, the more confused he felt. He got out his notepad and tried to make sense of it all. An hour later, he looked at the jumble of unanswered questions on the page in front of him. Oh well, he sighed, packing up to go home. What more can happen now?

Is Drusilla really guilty? Why would she risk ruining her career? Is her motive convincing? She wouldn't have had time to fuse the lights and do the strangling, so did she rely on chance? Or did she have an accomplice? Is she the person most likely to have had access to a Mythikan poison? When could she have sawn through the light ropes? (Not while Minnie and I were in the studio - she was in her dressing room.) And what about Will Pry's evidence against her? Is it really conclusive?

1) Strangling. Haphazard.
Relied on chance light fusing. If it didn't, two people must have been involved - one to fuse lights, other to strangle.

2) Poison. Painstakingly planned.
Will Pry had it examined: some kind of Mythikan poison. Who would have access to it? Need to plan carefully to get hold of. Would have succeeded if Bella hadn't objected to her lines. Cup filled at 9am. Cat died at 9:10, so only ten possible minutes. All Workout team could have done it. Who had most opportunity? Would anyone have found it easy to do without being noticed?

3) Arc light. Risky.
No real guarantee of when light would fall and that it would definitely land on Bella.

Could the noise Minnie and I heard in the roof have been the villain at work on the light? If so, can we eliminate anyone as not being villain - was anyone definitely not up in roof at the time?

Seem to be three very different kinds of murder attempts. Not much in common. None of them would be guaranteed of success.
Could there be another link between them apart from Bella as victim? And why is Bella the victim anyway - who would have a grudge against her? Seem quite dramatic, showy sorts of crimes. Does that tell me anything about the kind of person that might have planned them?

What about the things in Minnie's bag? Would it help to look at them again?
Subway ticket: station name partly obscured by ink blot. Should I try and work out what station name is? Is the date important?
Moves and Grooves clipping. What does the message mean? Who wrote it?
Personal ad. Why does it seem so familiar?

THE PHOTOS - WHY, WHY, WHY would anyone steal them? And why is one still missing?

Vanishing Act

The big day had dawned at last. The evening would be filled with the excitement and glitter of the Bravos. But now it was cold and foggy. It was still early and most of the streets were silent and deserted. Only a few shops were beginning to open their shutters as Jack set off, bleary-eyed, for the Workout studio.

Speeding along in an uptown train, Jack fretted once more over the arrest of Drusilla Dazzle. But he soon had something else to think about. Outside the Qualivision building a huge crowd of reporters was gathered around the steps, hurling questions at the security guard: "Any news?" "Any comment?" "Any idea where he might be?"

Jack was bewildered. What were they all talking about? Just then a news vendor shouted out: "Workout star in no-show drama! Read all about it!" Jack fumbled for some change and grabbed a copy of the paper. Staring out from the front page was a very familiar face.

Luke in his first TV role, as Kid Cop.

A close friend commented, "It seems most unlike Luke. He is always so reliable." He was seen leaving the Qualivision building yesterday afternoon, clutching a copy of Qualitime, and muttering, "No more! No more!" Friends are at a loss to explain this comment.

The last reported sighting of Luke Martin was in Queen Street by little Frank Donaldson. The tiny tot was crying because his kite was stuck in a tree when the star passed by. Living up to his athletic TV image, Luke vaulted high up into the tree, then walked along a narrow branch as easily as if he was on the ground. He untangled the kite then shinned down the tree and ran off, obviously in a hurry.

Little Frankie Donaldson – the last person to have seen Luke Martin?

Daily Tittle Tattle

MISSING! TOP STAR IN REAL LIFE DRAMA

TV heart-throb Luke Martin in his current role as athlete Dan Drummond in Workout.

News came in late last night of the sudden mystery disappearance of Luke Martin, young star of top TV show, Workout. The teen idol was due to turn up yesterday evening at the Yahboos, the music industry's answer to TV's Bravos, to present the award for best new act to young band, Glug. He never arrived. Speculation is growing as to his whereabouts. For full story, see back page.

Luke missing! It was almost impossible to believe. Aghast, Jack hurried up the steps. The security guard recognized him and waved him through. Inside studio 3, everyone seemed to be in a state of shock.

It was all too much for the stricken cast and crew of Workout. They seemed unable to think of what to do next. But just then the door burst open and in marched Will Pry. He looked very grim-faced indeed as he started to speak.

The private eye took a sheet of paper out of the envelope he was brandishing. Everyone crowded around to read it.

By the time you read this I will be thousands of miles away. Do not try to find me. Someone there will understand what I'm doing and why.

I confess to my part in the crimes against Bella. Drusilla is innocent of everything. I never dreamed things would go this far. I am despicable, but even I have a point at which I must stop. I will do no more. I have done enough already.

Luke Martin

It certainly made for some very interesting reading. You could have heard a pin drop while they took in what it said.

On with the Show!

After the first shocked reactions, the voices died away. No one could believe what they had just read. It seemed too incredible. Then Thea broke the silence. "So, Drusilla is innocent. She must be released at once!"

"It's all in hand," said Will Pry. He seemed a little edgy. "The lady should be here any time now. I wasted no time in getting her release once the letter arrived." Tugging down his hat, he turned to the door. "Anyway, I gotta scram," he continued. "Thanks to my efforts, the notorious Spotlight Gang are cooling their heels in a cold cell. They're in need of some serious questioning." With that, he turned up his collar and left the studio fast.

Minnie tugged on Jack's sleeve. "Listen! I have some vital information," she said urgently. "It was when I saw Pawprint's rug, that was when I knew. And I was right!" But Jack was listening to raised voices in the corridor outside the studio. The door flew open.

"Drusilla!" gasped everyone, as she burst into the room, seemingly unbowed by the shattering experiences of the last twenty-four hours.

"I'm back!" announced the star. "And just in time to spot that fool of a detective slinking away down the corridor. Imbecile!" She paused dramatically. "And now to work!"

"But Luke played a big part in the scene. Can we get something else ready in time? We have nothing prepared," said Thea doubtfully.

Fraser had been writing feverishly ever since Will Pry had told them the news of Drusilla's release. Now it was his turn to speak. "Let's turn this disaster into triumph!" he declared, jumping up and waving a script around. "We'll give the Bravos a scene to remember. We'll make it really dramatic, give Drusilla the central role," continued the scriptwriter, his eyes aglint with excitement. Then he began to explain his idea to a spellbound audience.

Never were lines learned so quickly! They rehearsed the scene again and again until, at last, Thea was satisfied. "Congratulations, cast," she beamed. "Tonight, the show will go on after all!"

26

Everyone cheered. Only Drusilla seemed deep in thought, speaking so quietly that only Jack could hear. "It's ten years," she murmured. "But I'm almost sure . . ."

And there's the ring as well.

Please listen to me!

What was she talking about? Jack was filled with a deep sense of foreboding. Then Minnie pressed something into his hand. The missing photo!

"Just look at the time," Thea exclaimed, looking up with a gasp. "Only four hours until the Bravos!" Jack followed her gaze up to the clock perched above the phone booth, then he glanced back down at the photo. All at once, he realized exactly why it had been so important for someone to conceal it. And the proof was right here in his hand.

Race Against Time

Time was running out. Ignoring Minnie's pleading behind him, Jack raced out of the studio. Next stop was the Qualitime office.

Up three flights of stairs and along a corridor that seemed to stretch for miles, at last he reached the offices of the Qualivision daily newspaper. Seated behind a large desk was a portly receptionist. His eyebrows shot up as Jack explained what he wanted.

. . . back issues from ten years ago . . . and last week . . . phone record . . . personal ads . . .

TOP OF THE FLOPS

We had no idea what we were starting when we invited you to nominate your worst show this year from stage, screen or TV. Your nominations came flooding in.

Today we can reveal that the runaway winner, with over one-third of all the votes cast, was

DREAMAWAY! A stage spectacular that fizzled out after just one night.

Drusilla Dazzle in the worst career move of her life. Will she recover from this disaster? One thing's for sure, her co-star won't - she's made sure of that!

Bob Swing, taking his first and last step into the limelight. What will he do now? Time for a career change, Bob!

By now, the whole story of the disastrous first and last night of the musical tragedy, Dreamaway, has gone down into theatrical folklore. Those of you who were there say it is a night you will never forget - largely due to the efforts of one man, Bob Swing. In his role as the Dream Maker, he managed to turn the evening into a nightmare for the cast. Even a seasoned old pro like Drusilla couldn't hold the show together. Unfortunately, what was meant to be a tragedy turned into a comedy, with most of the audience hysterical with laughter. But no one in the cast was chuckling when the reviews came out the next day and closed the show.

From list of phone calls to Qualitime Personal column. This proves a call was made from studio 3.

Friday, October 16

Outside number: 603860013
Time: 2:51
Length of call: 8 mins

Internal number: 254 (Studio 3)
Time: 3:00pm
Length of call: 6 mins

Outside number: 701731222
Time: 3:07pm
Length of call: 2 mins

Internal number: 171 (Accounts)
Time: 3:09pm
Length of call: 3 mins

Internal number: 409 (Personnel)
Time: 3:23pm
Length of call: 5 mins

Outside number: 808174983
Time: 3:34pm
Length of call: 13 mins

From the record of ads taken for Qualitime Personal column.

Day	Date	Method	Time
Friday	Oct 16	Hand delivered	2:40

Message:
Amelia. Come to a party at my house tonight. I shall cook you a meal to remember.

Day	Date	Method	Time
Friday	Oct 16	Phoned	3:00

Message:
Remember the Mythikan kidnap? I know who you are, 'Dan'. I will tell all unless you do as I say. I shall call you tonight. Make sure you are home.

Day	Date	Method	Time
Friday	Oct 16	Hand delivered	3:10

Message:
Visit Chuckles 'n' Chocs for novelty gift ideas for the star 'who has everything'.

It took a while to convince the bemused receptionist to help. But at last, an hour on, Jack was armed with all the information he needed. Then he raced downtown to the Informer office. Sitting at his desk, he hurriedly laid everything out in front of him.

I only hope I'm not too late. This may be a matter of life and death!

Let's check I'm right first, he thought. There are things I still need to puzzle out. I must be sure before I act.

Remember the Mythikan kidnap? I know who you are, 'Dan'. I will tell all unless you do as I say. I shall call you tonight. Make sure you are home.

'Dan'. Instructions are where I told you. Follow them exactly. Don't fail me or I shall be forced to talk to the police.

'Dan'. This time more complicated. Two job for you. New instructions in the same place. Don't fail me or you know what will happen.

'Dan'. Hello again! Another little task for you. Make sure you carry it out. Instructions are in the same place.

From last Monday's issue. Could it be useful?

IN THE PIPELINE
From Sam Smarm, Publicity Department

Exciting news! Qualivision plans to make a miniseries of the Minnie Marvel kidnap. We have no word yet of who is up to play the major roles. Little Minnie is, of course, now too old to play herself as a three-year-old.

Hotly tipped for the role of Minnie's mother is Bella Bouquet. When Minnie was asked her opinion, she said "Bella would be good. She reminds me of my mother. They have the same sort of smile and they laugh the same way."

As far as actors to play the members of the notorious kidnap gang, only a stunt man has been chosen so far. He will be needed for the dramatic final rescue scene where little Minnie is carried to safety by one of her kidnappers. In an accurate reconstruction of the real rescue, the stunt man will have to carry Minnie (a dummy will be used) over a narrow tree lodged between two sides of a waterfall. One false move and the stunt man will hurtle thousands of feet down into the fast-flowing Intrepid River.

One wag in our department has suggested that Luke Martin would be ideally suited to the role. With his childhood background of circus skills we might even save on the stunt man fee!

By the time he had finished reading, his worst suspicions were confirmed. Minnie had given him the one vital piece of evidence that proved his story – the photo. But where on earth could she have found it?

Quaking at the thought of what he had to do, Jack jumped up. There was no time to worry about that now. If his guess was right, the villain had one last dastardly act planned, a fiendish crime that would take place this very evening in front of thousands and be beamed live to countless watching nations around the globe. Somehow, the Bravos must be stopped!

The Final Countdown

At that moment, Ed Lines walked in. "What's up, kid?" he asked, seeing Jack's worried face.

"There's going to be a murder at the Bravos," burbled Jack. "Unless we stop it. But how can we get there in time? And –"

"Whoa," said Ed. "Start again, and this time, make sense." Then he listened while Jack told his story. When Jack had finished, Ed looked at his watch. "We have forty-five minutes," he said. "To the Bravos – and fast!" And so began a frantic race against time . . .

STOP! DON'T TURN THE PAGE YET. You now have all the information you need to solve the string of dastardly doings. Can you reveal the identity of the fiendish felon?

Under the Spotlight

Drusilla screamed. Startled, Rock jerked the gun up to the ceiling. There was a deafening crack, then the auditorium was plunged into darkness.

Seconds later, the beam of a spotlight started to rove around the room. It swept up to the balcony and came to rest on Jack. All eyes turned to him. "Drusilla Dazzle," he began. "Someone loaded the gun intending that you should die tonight. That person was Fraser Storey!"

Gasps could be heard all around the auditorium. Jack pressed on. "Why should Fraser want to harm you? Because he is none other than Bob Swing, the actor who ten years ago starred with you in Dreamaway, and ruined the show with his incompetence. You made sure he never acted again, so he vowed revenge – and tonight he very nearly got it."

"But Bella . . ." began Drusilla.

"Fraser staged the attempts on Bella's life too," Jack cut in. "He didn't really want to kill her at all; he wanted to frame you as the would-be murderer and see you sent to prison. When his plans failed, he decided to turn to murder himself!"

Suddenly, a voice cut through the darkness. "An interesting theory, young man," said Fraser Storey. "But tell me, do you actually have any proof for your fanciful accusations?"

"I most certainly do," said Jack, pulling something from his pocket. "You gave yourself away when you chose an accomplice for your crimes."

"You found out that Luke Martin had been in the Spotlight Gang and used blackmail threats to force him to help you. Those ads you put in Qualitime for him to see – I knew they had something to do with the attempts on Bella's life. I saw in the company log when the calls had been made to place the ads. But it wasn't until I saw the photo of Friday's rehearsal which showed you making a call that I had proof that you were the culprit. The photo matched the time and number in the company log. After that, everything fell into place."

"Not so fast," said the voice from the darkness. "You may have your proof – but I have a hostage!" The spotlight swung around to reveal the frightened face of Minnie Marvel. "Yes Drusilla, I did want my revenge," continued Fraser, enjoying his moment of power. "Just because I had stage fright and forgot my lines, you made sure my career was over. So I formed my plan – I would ruin you as you had ruined me."

"I didn't know why you seemed so familiar," said Drusilla in wonder. "Then your ring jogged my memory. You always used to wear it . . ."

"The strangling attempt was meant to frame you," interrupted Fraser. "Pawprint's poisoning, too. I knew Bella would object to that scene. How simple to drop poison in the glass and break it while demonstrating her new lines! The arc light was risky, but I was ready when it fell to make sure no one was harmed. And it was easy to plant the evidence when I went to your dressing room with Will Pry."

"Then there was Luke." Fraser was unable to stop now. "He got involved with the Spotlight Gang but left as soon as he could. He was the one who rescued Minnie. Shame he can't do it again, eh?" He smiled as he tightened his grip on the little girl. "Luke moved to Los Tamillion and thought he was safe. The only photo of the gang the police had was so blurred he thought no one would ever know. How sad for him that I visited my sister Elsa – the plastic surgeon who operated on the gang – and found she had a photo that showed him clearly. So I contacted him. What a waste of time he was . . ."

All is Revealed

Thump! Thud! Crash! The sounds of a tremendous scuffle echoed down from the lighting gallery. The lights flooded on and feet thundered down the stairs. Then Fraser Storey appeared, dragging Minnie Marvel, and with Luke Martin in hot pursuit. Luke flung himself forward and hurled Fraser to the ground. "Gotcha!" Luke gasped. "I knew I was right to come back!"

"You again!" shouted Fraser. "You've ruined everything –" He drummed his fists on the floor in frustration.

"If only I'd thrown away those photos," he sniffed. "I tore them up and threw them away, then I panicked. Suppose someone found the vital one? So I stuffed all the pieces of it – except one bit that I couldn't find in time – into Pawprint's basket. I planned to destroy them later."

"But someone else got to that vital photo before you did," Jack pointed out. "Minnie Marvel."

Minnie beamed proudly. "I knew something was in Pawprint's basket," she explained. "His rug was all messed up."

"Foiled by a child!" muttered Fraser through gritted teeth.

"Fraser Storey, I have heard everything," said Will Pry, emerging from the audience, with two police officers following. "I arrest you for . . ."

"Stop!" interrupted Drusilla. "I am not blameless in all this. I have long regretted ruining Fraser's acting career as I did. And now, thanks to his scripts, Rock and I are working together again after so many wasted years. That is worth more to me than anything else. Fraser, I shall not press charges!"

Fraser looked up, astonished. Tears of gratitude began to stream down his face. Just then, a quiet voice said, "Errr, what about me?"

It was Luke. He looked nervous. Then Will Pry spoke. "Your heroic action today and your role in the Minnie Marvel kidnap rescue should excuse you from prosecution," he said. The gripped Bravos audience gave a loud cheer.

Meanwhile, Ed Lines turned to Bella Bouquet and held out his hands. "Daughter dear, I'm sorry for our silence of the last two years. I realize that acting is the right thing for you. Will you forgive me, Arabella? I know now that not everyone can want to be a reporter."

"But *I* do," chirped a small voice behind him. Minnie babbled on but Ed was staring at her arm. "How did you get that scar?" he asked.

"In an accident when I was three," said Minnie. "I got my arm stuck in some guttering." To everyone's astonishment Ed Lines burst into tears. "Then you must be my long-lost niece!" he sobbed.

Just then, Will Pry's phone rang. He listened intently then spoke, beaming. "A woman has been found up the Intrepid River. She says she fell over a cliff four years ago and was rescued by mountain yetis. She has lived with them ever since and only just recovered her memory. Her name is Christabel Lines!"

Detective Guide

This page will give you some help in solving the case. The numbers written here refer to the numbers inside the magnifying glasses found throughout the book.

1 Take your time over this. It could prove useful later. Don't forget to look at the pictures closely.
2 This could be worth studying carefully.
3 Take a good look at this scene.
4 Keep your eyes open and listen carefully to Thea.
5 Listen hard here. Some of this may not mean much now, but try to remember it.
6 There are some interesting reactions to the sight of those photos.
7 There's more to this page than might first appear.
8 So everyone has chosen an outfit for the Bravos – or have they? Are you sure?
9 It could be a good idea to make a note of those opening times.
10 There may be some enlightening new information here. Read everything carefully.
11 The pictures may lend a hand here.
12 Look closely at this page, then think hard about what – and whom – you have seen.
13 Can you sort out the information to see which bits are useful?
14 Jack's notepad may be more helpful than he realizes.
15 A tragic tale indeed. Keep your eyes and ears peeled.
16 Rats – or could it be something else?
17 Those sort of doors don't blow open, do they? So what's the alternative?
18 This page could be very revealing. It might help if you work out who all the handwriting belongs to.
19 You too could take a good look at the shrine to the feline fatality. Has anything changed?
20 A very lucky escape indeed – or was it?
21 Will Pry may be closer to the real truth than he knows, but perhaps he is looking at things from the wrong angle.
22 It might help to take another look at the pile of information Ed Lines first gave to Jack.
23 It is worth trying to answer as many of these questions as you can.
24 Does anything in this article trigger off any memories of another dramatic incident in the past?
25 Keep your ears open here.
26 Listen hard to what Drusilla is saying.
27 By now your brain should be starting to tick . . .
28 Are things becoming clearer? If not, try looking back at pages 7 and 9 for more help.
29 A grudge – against whom?

By the Way

Now you've read the story and solved the mystery, check whether you spotted every clue. If you have difficulty reading this try holding the page in front of a mirror.

Did you notice that Pawprint's blanket was all scrunched up on page 30 – something the feline megastar would never have allowed (see page 8). And did you guess that Fraser had put the missing photo in there? That was why he kept trying to move the basket later, searching for a chance to get the photo out and throw it away safely. Did you spot that Fraser's ring was the same as the one worn by Bob Swing? It first appeared on page 7, then throughout the book. It should have given you a clue that they were the same person. And did you spot Fraser's handwriting on the script and the news clipping on page 29?

There were lots of clues to the identity of the mystery kidnapper who left the Spotlight Gang. Jack's notebook on page 24 mentioned that Luke's parents had a circus trapeze and high wire act that Luke joined. No wonder he was able to run along a narrow branch over a waterfall in the dramatic rescue of Minnie Marvel! His agile rescue of Frankie Donaldson's kite on page 36 was another clue. On page 41, there was a final big hint in the news from Sam Smarm in the Publicity Department of Qualivision.

Did you work out the blackmail plot? On page 10, Thea mentioned Fraser's recent visit to his sister, and if you weren't sure that she was Elsa Storey, the Qualitime quiz confirmed it. All the ads in Qualitime were addressed to 'Dan' – Luke's name in Workout. On page 11 Thea mentioned how bad Luke's acting had been that Monday – the day he would have read the first ad in Qualitime. And on page 35, Jack's notebook mentions that the poison is Mythikan. The two people with a Mythikan connection were Fraser and Luke.

There were plenty of clues that Fraser stole the photos. First, there was his leaking pen. If you look closely at the subway ticket to Paparazzi Park station, you will see an ink blot on that, too. And Fraser was the only person who would have had time to get to the printers before they closed. Did you work out that Bella was Ed's daughter, Arabella, by his marriage to actress Posy Bouquet (see page 7)? So that would explain his choice of headlines on page 34!

First published in 1994 by Usborne Publishing Ltd, Usborne House, 83-85 Saffron Hill, London EC1N 8RT, England.

Printed in Great Britain U.E.
First published in America August 1994